Emma Lou and the Reindeer Flu

Dear Santa,

story and drawings by J.H. Stroschin

© J. H. STROSCHIN - Henry Quill Press - 1998
7340 Lake Drive, Fremont, MI 49412

ISBN:1-883960-15-0

and special thanks to Cyndi and Frank

for my family

Emma Lou was eagerly awaiting Santa Claus. This year she hoped he would bring her a doll. A doll which she had described very carefully in her letter to him.

Dear Santa,
    Please bring me a doll.
A lovely lady in an apron and a shawl, with braided dark hair and bright smart eyes on a smiling face.
    She would look like Mama, at least, that is what Gramma Emma said.
    Thank you. Love, Emma Lou
P.S. Please bring more yarn for Gramma.

Every year Gramma Emma asked for the same thing. Yarn. Yarn to knit mittens and scarves to give away to folks.

Emma Lou and Gramma lived on a small farm with their animals. Emma Lou enjoyed taking care of her farm friends.

Each day Emma Lou cared for Beans the pig, Red the chicken and Waddles the duck, who all needed their corn bowls filled. Minnie the sheep, Molly the cow and Curlie the donkey were expecting their fresh hay. Tonight, the cat and dog, Fluffy and Fred were also waiting for their dinners. However, Emma Lou was so excited, she could not think about corn and hay. She kept walking to the barn door to look out.

It was Christmas Eve!

Even the animals knew something special would happen tonight.

Emma Lou saw Fred's ears perk up and his head tilt to one side. A moment later she heard it too. Softly at first:

JINGLE JANGLE JINGLE JANGLE

. . . then louder . . .

JINGLE JANGLE JINGLE JANGLE

"Oh Gramma," she said, "He's here! Santa Claus is here!"
The roof of their home was too small for the sleigh to land, so Santa chose an open space in front of the barn.

While wrapping herself in her mother's old shawl, Emma Lou joyously ran toward him. Gramma Emma followed closely behind her.

"Oh, my! Oh, mercy!" moaned Santa as he scurried from reindeer to reindeer.

"Oh, my! Oh, mercy! Oh, dear!!"

Dasher and Dancer were coughing and sneezing.
Prancer and Vixen were hacking and wheezing.
Comet and Cupid were sniffling and groaning.
While Donner and Blitzen were shivering and moaning.

"They were healthy when we left the North Pole," sighed Santa. "All these presents to deliver and the reindeer are too sick to pull my sleigh. What ever will I do?"

Gramma Emma insisted, "No time to worry now. We must get them into the warm barn."

As they walked to the barn, the only sounds to be heard were:

Cough! Sneeze! Sniff! Wheeze!

Ah-Choo!

"Whatever will I do?" moaned Santa.
Emma Lou thought for a moment. Then she tugged on Santa's coat and asked, "If the magic of Christmas can make reindeer fly, why not take our farm animals? They would make a great team!"

"But . . . but they are not reindeer. Reindeer are supposed to pull my sleigh! Reindeer have always pulled my sleigh!" answered Santa Claus.

"Well Santa," laughed Gramma Emma, "look at it this way, these animals are healthy and they're here; and, so is Christmas Eve. What else can you do?"

Santa thought for a moment. Then he tugged on his beard.

"Ho! Ho! Ho!" he laughed, " Of course! That is a splendid idea.
Let's hitch up our new team and take to the sky.
Your idea has saved me. Ho! Ho! Ho!"

As Santa climbed into his sleigh, he called to his new team,

"On Beans!   On Minnie!
On Molly!   On Fred!
On Curlie!   On Fluffy!
On Waddles!   On Red!"

And, off they flew. What a curious sight and sound it was:

JINGLE   JANGLE Oink–Oink, Moo!
JINGLE   JANGLE Hee–Haw, Woof!
JINGLE   JANGLE Baa–Baa, Meoowww!
JINGLE   JANGLE Cluck–Cluck, QUACK!

Gramma Emma and Emma Lou stood in the barnyard watching Santa disappear into the night sky.

"Oh Gramma!" Emma Lou 's joy at helping Santa, suddenly turned into despair.

"Oh Gramma, he forgot my doll!" Now with tears on her cheeks, "Oh Gramma, your yarn. He forgot that, too!"

From the sky they could hear:

> *JINGLE JANGLE* Oink–Oink, Moo!
> *JINGLE JANGLE* Hee–Haw, Woof!
> *JINGLE JANGLE* Baa–Baa, Meoowww!
> *JINGLE JANGLE* Cluck–Cluck, QUACK!

From the barn they could hear:

> "Cough!" "Sneeze!" "Sniff!" "Wheeze!"
>
> **"AH-CHOOO!"**

"No time for tears," Gramma said with a hug and a kiss, "We have sick reindeer to tend. So boil some water while I make a special tea. And bring all of our mittens, scarves, and quilts for them. They are looking rather chilled."

All night Gramma and Emma Lou cared for the sick reindeer.

How confused Emma Lou felt. Happy to help Santa Claus. Sad because he forgot her doll. Angry to be stuck here in the barn, and not in her cabin, playing with a new doll by the warm fireplace.

"I'm tired of tending sick reindeer," complained Emma Lou. "This is not exactly how I expected to spend Christmas Eve!"

As Gramma handed Emma Lou another bucket of tea she smiled gently and said, "My dear child, Christmas isn't about what you get. I'm sure you already know the real joy of Christmas."

Emma Lou thought about what Gramma Emma just said. The joy of Christmas is about giving. And, the more she helped the reindeer, the happier she felt. "Santa will be happy too," she thought. "Just think Gramma, we'll give a present to Santa! We'll give him healthy reindeer for his ride home."

"That is the spirit Emma Lou," said Gramma.

All night they made tea and cared for the reindeer. Finally, too tired to fill even one more bucket with tea, Emma Lou and Gramma Emma fell asleep on a small pile of straw.

"Cough!" "Sneeze!" "Sniff!" "Wheeze!"

"AH-CHOOO!"

were the last sounds the heard as they drifted off to sleep.

Gramma Emma and Emma Lou never heard the approaching sounds of

JINGLE JANGLE Oink–Oink, Moo!
JINGLE JANGLE Hee–Haw, Woof!
JINGLE JANGLE Baa–Baa, Meoowww!
JINGLE JANGLE Cluck–Cluck, QUACK!

As the early sun rose pink in the sky, Gramma Emma and Emma Lou woke slowly to the sound of

"Cock–a–doodle–doo–oo–o!"

The old rooster announced the beginning of a new day.

No sounds of:

"Oink–Oink, Moo–oo–o!"
"Hee–Haw, Woof!"
"Baa–Baa, Meow!"
        or
"Cluck, Cluck, QUACK!"

were heard, for these animals
were all sleeping very soundly.

"Oh Gramma, this straw is so soft, I could sleep here all day," yawned Emma Lou.

This straw is unusually soft thought Gramma Emma, as she rubbed her eyes, yawned and stretched.

"Oh my! Oh mercy! Oh dear!" laughed Gramma Emma. "Look Emma Lou open your sleepy eyes! This isn't straw!"

They were lying on yarn! Yarn from all over the world. Yarn from the sheep of Scotland and New Zealand. Yarn from the alpaca and llama of South America. Yarn from the angora goats of the Himalayas.

Yarn! Yarn! And more yarn!

But most importantly,

on top of the yarn lay the most beautiful doll with an apron, a shawl, braided dark hair, and bright smart eyes on a smiling face.

Gramma Emma hugged Emma Lou. Emma Lou hugged Gramma Emma and held her doll tightly in her arms.

"She looks just like your Mama," whispered Gramma Emma.

MERRY CHRISTMAS